CW00872217

A Collection of Monster Stories

5AIR

Compiled and edited for print

by RM Morrissey

Written by students

First Published 2021 by RM Morrissey

ISBN: 9798518002722

Copyright © RM Morrissey, 2021

The right of the authors within this collection of works have been asserted in accordance with the Copyright, Designs and Patents Act, 1988.

All rights reserved. No part of this publication may be reproduced, stored in a retrieval system, or transmitted, in any form or by any means (electronic, mechanical, photocopying, recording or otherwise), without the prior written permission of the publisher.

To all the hard working students and teachers who make writing happen.

Forward

Dear Reader,

In this book you will find a bunch of stories written by year five students.

This year we studied Robert Nye's *Beowulf* and wrote a collection of stories that had a similar idea. A battle of good vs evil, right vs wrong, heroes vs monsters. That said, not all of our students wanted to go for a classic ending where the good guy wins. Some of these stories have brutal twists which will leave you feeling like all hope is lost. In others, you'll think that all hope is lost and then BAM! Somehow the hero pulls it out of the bag, clutching victory from the jaws of defeat. And some of them borrow from Nye's gruesome imagination, leaving the reader feeling quite disgusted.

All of our students worked hard and enjoyed writing their short stories. I hope that seeing their work in print will inspire some of them to continue building their imaginations and to continue to foster their writing skills.

It has been a pleasure reading and editing these stories for print.

I hope you enjoy these stories as much as I did - even the gross ones!

RM Morrissey

A Wolf and Its Pigs

By: RM Morrissey

It's not the wolf you should fear in the woods.

Once upon a time, in the beautiful meadows near Hall Heorot, there lived three little pigs who had set out to build homes of their own. Their mother had told them before they set out on their adventure to build strong, sturdy homes for they never know what might come knocking during the night. The two younger pigs scoffed at their mother's advice and built rickety homes of straw and wood for they were lazy and wanted to pass the day indulging in mud baths and scarfing down mounds of food and barrels of drink. However, the eldest was much wiser and heeded his mother's words. He built a sturdy home of brick and stone - one which would hold back the creatures which wandered at night.

Away off in the distance, sunken in the shadows of Hall Heorot, was a black, wicked fen, steeped in darkness and blood. All manner of vile and wretched creatures stalked around in the gloom, seeking things to devour. It is from here that a lone wolf emerged, hoping for an easy snack. That wolf was one of the weakest, one of the scrawniest creatures in that pit of evil and would sooner be eaten than eat if he were to stay there while the sun is set.

It wasn't long before the wolf found the tiny, straw home of the first little pig. With a wicked laughter and hoarse voice he spat, "Here little piggy. Here little piggy. Why don't you come out and play? I'm hungry and you'd make such a fine dinner."

As he heard the wolf take in a deep breath, the pig replied in a panicked voice, "Not by the hair on my chinny, chin-chin!" But just as he finished speaking, the wolf had blown his house apart and the pig went squealing to his brother's stick home for safety.

The wolf was furious that his dinner had run away so he followed and found the tiny, shabbily-built, stick house of the second pig. With that same hoarse laughter, the wolf whispered through the gaps in the sticks, "Little piggies, little piggies, you really should come out and play, for if you don't, I'll huff and I'll puff and I'll blow these sticks away!" Now the wolf didn't give the pigs time to react and just blew the house apart only to find that the pigs had already fled to their older brother's sturdy, brick and stone house.

The wolf approached this home and began to slump for he knew that no matter how hard he blew, or how hard he scratched and clawed at the door, he would never be able to get inside. He sulked and turned back towards the edges of the fen, hoping he could stay safe and maybe catch a squirrel or a rat to feed his rumbling belly.

The pigs stood at their lit window and laughed at the wolf singing, "Who's afraid of a big, bad wolf? No, no, no, not us!" They sang and they laughed; they ate and they drank; and were so full of happiness and glee throughout the night. But little did they know that the sounds of their celebration had carried out across the meadow and stirred something dark, something wicked, something truly evil in the depths of the fen.

From the darkest part of the fen, from the deepest, darkest pools which led straight to hell, came a creature unlike anything the world had ever seen. It had fierce, red eyes glowing in the darkness. It had red, sharp claws that could tear their victims limb from limb. It had scummy, scabby lips dripping with blood and gore.

That monster moved slowly, like a snake stalking its prey. It crawled towards the little pig's house, dragging its enormous, fat, swollen body through the pools of blood and mounds of twisted, broken bodies - half eaten upon the ground. As the monster slithered towards the happy singing of the little pigs, it heard something revolting, something far worse than those three pigs. Hall Heorot was in a blaze of light with hundreds of people singing and dancing and laughing. The monster, with pure hatred burning in its eyes, turned towards Hall Heorot – towards that which it hated most above all.

The Battle of Life

By: Rodela

"Kaitlin Newman!"

Oh, that's Mum, she promised me the entire, whole evening to myself if I did my homework now. But first I'll tell you what happened a few days ago.

I had finished college and was walking home while reading, "The Caladwar Quests: Tangled Time" when I realised, by accident, I was walking into the abandoned, desolate graveyard that apparently nobody had been in for years and years. I had always been scared of this graveyard in particular. I used to tiptoe precariously whenever I passed it, horrendously afraid that a rotting corpse would pop out of its grave and grab me by the ankles! I wondered if that absurd, nonsensical thing could ever happen to me in real life. I'm not a kid anymore, I'm well older than five now. I'm seventeen! I shouldn't be afraid of such things.

I suppose I should tell the inquisitive, curious readers, "What I am like." I like to read interesting and intriguing books and do amazingly artistic art and I have a strange and odd knack of swallowing down facts as if they were sweets and passing exams like I'm playing a game with my friends. I have very prominent cheekbones and my eyes are large and often animated with barely any lashes at all. They're the colour of chestnuts mostly but are actually a hazelnut brown. My hair is oddly double-coloured black and brown, like a witch's. Anyway, I am training to go to either Oxford or Cambridge.

As I looked at these graves, I found quite a thoughtful epitaph about a six year old girl who lit up her parents' lives, Anastasia Hale. Sitting there, I could hear the deathly silence, the somber silence. Graveyards are supposed to be quiet but it seemed like a curtain of silence had wrapped itself around the entire place. All life had been drained from the graveyard, like water had been drained from a well. Birds were flying away from the place – one by one – in rapid succession. Even the graveyard should have some life in it, but somehow, someone made it like this.

Suddenly I heard a scream, a deathly scream, the cry of death. There was an almighty gasp and then silence, ghostly silence, deathly silence.

I went around the bush to see with a fright …

Oh.

A dead body lay in front of me. Someone was dead! Standing next to the corpse was a girl, a girl of eighteen, a girl of my age, and a girl of my age who had murdered someone. She had hair as black crow's feathers, piercing blue eyes, cold as ice. Her eyes were hell as she stared at me, looking through me, finding my weaknesses. She was tall and looked like a model; she had on a pink, ragged top and tight black leggings. Her carefully doll-featured face screamed malicious despite her cute attire.

"I freed him of the pains of life, now I'll free myself, Anastasia Hale!" Anastasia said menacingly. She had scars and cuts all over her face to mark all the victorious battles she had fought. Now, that just made me more scared!

"You are, you are, you are … the dead girl … from the … f-f-from the epitaph! W-w-what are you doing here? Back alive? You should be in your grave! B-b-but how?"

"I'm back to kill everyone else to repay for the pain I went through before passing away. When I passed, my parents were the only ones who were melancholy. Everyone else's life seemed unaffected! I have always believed that every person on Earth is to blame for my suffering and pain. You are also to blame for it, as innocent as you look!"

"How could you so cowardly believe I'm the reason you're suffering? Your time came for you to pass away and you clearly haven't taken it well. Nobody can be to blame for this, only you can fix the grave mistake you are about to make, not me. Your death was chosen for a reason and nobody on Earth chose it or could choose it." I said, stepping closer to her. There was no way I could run from her so I only had one choice.

I lunged at her, avenging the poor, unfortunate man on the gritty, gravelly ground. My arm grabbed instinctively for my penknife. Anastasia seemed to know how it went; her grey eyes flashed danger, amber like the rising sun, hoisting itself into the bright blue skies, like a boat floating out to sea. Just for a millisecond, I think I saw a glint of hesitation in her eyes.

I saw pain in her eyes, the want to be with her parents, the want to have a family again, the want to have friends, the want of everything the cup of life had from bottom to brim. Suddenly, she took a hard pound at my chest, catching me off guard. My heart was beating and hitting so hard in my chest, wanting to be let to rest and simply die, that I could actually hear it: da-dum, da-dum, da-dum. I shouted and yelped, Anastasia grinned and smiled. I grimaced and broke into a cold sweat.

She kicked me, not only with power, but also with grace, the work and gracefulness of a true master. I fell down. I was falling, falling, falling. I was dying, dying, dying. Was that my end? Was that what dying felt like?

Tayoma and his Monster Brother

By: Bushra

Long ago there was a land of Wealthies with a king named Daro. He had two sons named Chris and Tayoma. They had no mother. Their mother died when they were born Wealthies was a place of wealthy people. But … there was a house that was derelict next to a graveyard. It was called Dearies.

It was always be winter in Dearies, no one knew why. If the sun was out there were always black clouds covering it. On the right there was a graveyard, with broken stones of people's names. Some say one time a spirit even jumped out of his grave. Next to it, was a path that said, "The path of hell …"

Creepy, right?

Left to that path were street lights but not just normal street lights. These street lights had been on for one thousand years. What made those lights scary was that people had been hung on there! Next to those, was a river with poisonous, musty, thick water.

Many years later passed and Tayoma was sixteen years old, but sadly his brother got lost when they were ten. Chris had been missing for six years! People say he went to the Dearies. Tayoma was going on a mission to rescue his lost brother. And Tayoma wanted to see if he's still there. It took Tayoma a long time to get there, nearly a whole month, but finally, he reached the Dearies, wishing, hoping he would find his brother.

As soon as he reached the Dearies, he felt like the floor was shaking … and from the poisonous river, an enormous fifteen headed monster appeared. It was slimy, hideous and clearly poisonous.

It slowly crawled towards Tayoma, leaving red and green slime behind it. It had three heads on its neck and three more heads on his body with more heads instead of hair. It was slimy and abhorrent.

Tayoma was shocked and confused, he felt a shiver in his body. It felt like he knew the monster, like the monster was related to him somehow. A moment later he realised that, fifteen faces of that hideous monster were the same as his brother Chris. Tayoma had tears in his eyes …

Chris moved at Tayoma with inhuman ferocity as she didn't even recognise who Tayoma was. Tayoma felt like he's wasn't even Chris anymore but a monster wearing his skin. His hostility towards him was worrying Tayoma. Why did he hate Tayoma that much?

Chris attacked Tayoma like an angry lion. He attacked that monster with his red eyes giving him a dead stare, with his thirty eyes, trying to burn him dead! Suddenly Chris spit fire at Tayoma and the boy was burning to death. Taking his last breath, Tayoma said, "I love you brother and I always will." The whole world stopped. Birds stopped singing. Trees stopped growing. And Chris began to melt, melting the whole world with him. If Chris didn't go to the Dearies, the whole world would be still living. If Tayoma didn't have to take Chris from the Dearies the whole world would be breathing.

If only …

The Fight for a Cliff

By: Julia

Far away from England, was a land named Geat. Geat was a city and it had a prince, who was so wise and kind that no one would ever want to betray him. Tundra, roughly fifteen years old, was the name of the prince who ruled Geat and he had the biggest empire in the whole world.

Near the city Geat, was a beautiful cliff which was especially beautiful at midnight. Unfortunately, the cliff was ruled by an immense, black-hearted ice bird, and it was just as cruel as its heart. The bird would not let anyone go on their property, and if that ever happened, the bird would kill the person straight away.

Tundra did not like the fact that the cliff had to be ruled by a blasphemous creature so that's why he decided to go on an adventure to be the new owner of the cliff. He got his carriage ready and soon the vehicle was shining gold. It looked just like the sun!

Days and nights passed and the prince still wasn't at the top of the cliff. He thought it was some kind of curse from the ice bird. Though Tundra was right, it was a curse from the ice bird, he didn't give up so easily. Tundra eventually made it to the top of the cliff but now the problem was that it was one in the morning and the prince was very sleepy! But he couldn't take a break after all that travelling because he had a war to finish off. It was time he faced the bird ...

"Well, well, well, look who we have. Standing on my property, my cliff. What do you want, boy?" asked the ice bird.

"The land, please. You don't even care about it," said Tundra.

"I DO TAKE CARE OF MY CLIFF!" snapped the bird.

"I want to fight for it, alright? So is it a deal?" shouted Tundra.

"Deal, but trust me boy, you don't want to play with me ..." snarled the bird.

The battle began as soon as possible, and the worst thing about it was that the prince already had gashes and scars when it was only two seconds into the fight. Yes, it did look like Tundra was losing, but as the fight continued, it looked like he was starting to gain some weird powers. The bird pulled out his claws and tried to do another cut at Tundra – SLASH! The bird's tail was cut off by a sharp dagger.

The beast looked at the dagger that had cut off its tail – it thought that the dagger was as sharp as an ice shard! The creature was furious. It was so furious that even its feather colours started turning red like fire instead of blue like ice. It was so angry that now it was a fire bird.

Its head was flaming with fire and its horn was as red as lava. The beast was now so dangerous that one touch could burn you alive. Tundra was horrified. He was petrified. He wanted to run away. But he couldn't. He had to finish this fight once and for all. Before the fire bird could even attack, Tundra slashed the bird's eye off with his dual swords and SLASH! One eye was off and then soon the other one was off! After both eyes were slashed from the bird, it was completely blind. Now it was Tundra's chance to kill him. SLASH! The bird was dead. All of a sudden the bird's dead body started to vanish and dust came everywhere. Tundra defeated the bird. He was now the new owner of the cliff!

As soon as the people of Geat – or Geats because they lived in Geat – found out that their prince had beaten the bird, they were all shocked and surprised that a young boy could have so much strength inside him! Everyone started celebrating. First, a ball, then a party, next new buildings were built and last but not least, a crown for their prince was given as an offering to be the Geats' new king! Tundra accepted the offer and after some days, prince Tundra was crowned King

Tundra the Great.

Everyone lived happily for years with their new, beautiful cliff. But who knows what will happen in the future. That's the point. No one knows except for one person …

MY ADVENTURE!

By: Kya

Emerging in the deepest depths of England's most haunted graveyard and through the dead, skinny, naked trees surrounded with blood dripping skulls, lay the grey gravestone of Peter Haywood. When I went to look at his birthdate, I realised that it was painted in glittering, gold paint which made me think that he was very special or maybe even a celebrity that I haven't heard of before. But that wasn't the case. His birthdate said that he lived from 1802-2001, which meant he died at the age of 199! Later on, after exploring the horrific graveyard with fright in each step I took, I soon noticed that on Peter's gravestone it said that he had died from a heart attack.

Now that I had seen enough, I went to have a look at the gravestone next to Peter's which belonged to his sister Susan. I saw something in the corner of my eye. It was a hand! A hand coming from Peter's grave. I didn't think much of it at first because I thought it was a sculpture, until in a blink of an eye, the hand rose. It rose and then it jumped. It made me gag because of how disgusting things could actually be. It had boils as big as fingernails with dirt in a ring around it as well as veins of all sorts of colours such as pink, blue, purple and red with bruises all over.

Then, the hand stopped jumping. At that time I didn't hesitate. I just thought. I thought and thought and thought, trying to think of happy things! Children! I thought that if there had been children, this wouldn't even be a graveyard. It would be a playground with slides and swings and roundabouts. If there had been sunlight, the graveyard wouldn't be such an ugly, gloomy, somber place. It would in fact be a very happy place with no dead trees. If there weren't so many dead people, this graveyard wouldn't have so many gravestones. This thinking about happy things didn't work because when I opened my eyes, none of those things were there.

I remembered a story I hear once about this place. A rumour I guess. It was said that this graveyard had once been a very gorgeous meadow but there was an evil witch that cursed it. She did this because she had lost a loved one and she was starting to feel depressed. She thought that if she could no longer see her loved one then nobody could. It was the meadow she decided to curse because it was the most beautiful and most popular thing she could think of.

Snapping back to reality I saw the hand was still there. Since the hand hasn't moved yet, I had no reason to hesitate until I saw the weirdest thing and now I can't unsee it. Coming from Peter's sister's grave was a body full of scars and wounds, gashes and scratches. IT WAS PETER'S SISTER LUCY! Lucy chased me for ten minutes straight waiting to kill me, but luckily I found shelter. It wasn't much later where I heard a voice. I peeped round the corner with fright after every blink I took, thinking that someone would come out. No one did so I took another step until I saw someone. He looked like he was twenty but he had the exact same hands as I saw earlier coming from Peter's grave!

"Yes Tom. It is Peter Haywood," it said to me.

I was silent standing with horror in my eyes, thinking, "No way ..."

"You've come here to fight haven't you?"

He came running towards me with axes in both hands screaming, but I dodged his attack as swift as an eagle. Then, I ran towards him with a sword, but he got out his sword from who knows where and defended himself. He got out his shield from what felt like thin air and pushed me hard. I went flying across the graveyard. It took me about a minute to get up. I said to myself, still trying to catch my breath, "I can do this! Don't let him defeat you!"

I ran towards him with my sword and hit him again, and again, and again! I seemed to have closed my eyes while I was hacking at the man and when I opened them I saw that he was dead. He fell to my feet and began to turn to grey ash and dissolve back into the ground. I whispered to myself, "One monster down, where should I go next?"

The Unknown

By: Afrah

Emerging from the deepest depths of England and into the forbidden, blood curdling inhuman territory was a young boy, lost, alone, helpless. The boy's name was Adam. Adam was lost in a dead silent graveyard. If there had been noise, there would have been the crying and sobbing of the families. Not only was it silent, but it was also empty. This graveyard wasn't always silent and empty though. Instead, it was the opposite. It used to be a joyful village and everyone was always happy until one day an evil wizard cursed the village with a spell that no one could break. He turned it into a graveyard, and all the happy people died and were buried in the graves. Rumour has it that a creature haunts the graveyard and has stolen all of the dead bodies.

Adam, the young boy, was on his way to school when he saw builders re-arranging the pavement, so he had the idea of going through the graveyard. As he as walking through, he started wondering around and skipping and then started humming and then whistling. All of a sudden, a monster appeared. He had devil horns larger than an elephants tusks razor sharp, blunt claws and it also had twelve pack muscles wrapping around its body. It had a bloody tongue, scars, deep gashes, and it was big enough to hug an aero plane. Adam looked at it and he immediately realised that it wasn't a Halloween costume because it wasn't even October!

Before Adam could even realise what was going on, the monster grabbed a hold of him and started squeezing him. Luckily Adam knew Kung Foo and karate so he kicked the monster in the stomach. While the monster was crying and moaning about his stomach, Adam took a rock and threw it at the monsters head … and then … it fell. The monster fell. It was eliminated! Adam was so happy that he didn't even realise that the monsters body was gone. All that was left of him was his flesh and blood. But was he really dead? Was the monster actually eliminated? No one knows. No one will ever truly know …

Unknown Creature

By: Ashal

One day, in a dark forest, there was a creature with teeth as sharp as knives and nails as bloody as a vampire's lips.

Tom, who was a sixteen-year-old boy, lost his family because of that creature. He wanted to get revenge.

The monster lived in a cold place all alone and like Tom, it was sad because its family had also been killed, but by aliens. Due to this, the huge, malicious creature had killed Tom's family to try and make itself feel better. It didn't work and only caused more pain.

Eventually the creature and Tom came face to face with each other. Tom wanted revenge and instead of killing some random people like the creature choose to do, Tom was going to kill the creature which attacked his family. The creature began to come close to Tom and tried to bite him but Tom was quick! Tom got his sword out and slashed the creature's one leg off. With a slash the whole forest went silent for two seconds. Suddenly the monster kicked Tom into the mud with its other leg, getting him all muddy. Then the beast grew larger and shouted at Tom. While it shouted, Tom flew into a tree. The creature said, "I hope you had a nice life because today you will die." The creature bit Tom's head off. Blood poured all over the place making the grass bloody.

Tom was a fool to think he could beat such a monster by himself.

The Devil's Scorpion

By: Ella

A long time ago, in a far, far away land, there was an underground door. Someone decided to go in. This someone was a daredevil. Her name was Rose. Once she went in, she was teleported to a place called Hell. Rose decided to look around. When she looked behind, she saw something. It was the devil's pet, a huge scorpion. It was really terrifying.

It started to charge at her, but she dodged the attack. It got mad and set stuff on fire. Rose used her super speed and surrounded it. The creature got as mad as a lion and wasn't strong enough to win so it gave up and sent Rose back to Earth.

Rose was happy that she was able to defeat such a terrible creature. Her victory spread around the world and it seemed that there were no more villains as they were scared of Rose.

Every celebrated. Rose was their hero.

They all celebrated too soon though! The next day, the devil's pet arrived in her town. She had to fight it. Rose used her super speed again and defeated the devil's pet. Everyone in the town was joyful and busting with happiness again.

The Gates of Hell

By: Husna

Far away from where a creature lived, a boy named Mike was coming home from school. He had an idea to take a shortcut through the gloomy graveyard but when he stepped into it, he felt shiver down his spine. He saw dead pigeons scattered along the floor. "What the …" he whispered to himself.

Thinking that he was cool, Mike still went through the graveyard. Five minutes after walking, Mike heard a noise. "Is anybody there?" Mike questioned. There was no reply. He thought it was just a crow so he just left it. He got really scared because he heard different noises that scared him. Maybe he wasn't that cool. Maybe he shouldn't have taken this shortcut … Something or someone was following behind him. He was sure of it. He took a photo to check who was following behind him and you would not believe who it was. It was a lady with her hair down covering her face. Her hands were dirty and her long finger nails that had dirt underneath them were trying to reach up to Mike. She grabbed him and he was so scared that not even one inch of his body moved.

The GG man came to save him and the lady noticed the GG man was her dad. He noticed that the lady was his daughter as well. The GG man was so angry that his own daughter tried to kill him. She had killed her mother and tried to kill him, her father – Greg the GG man. Greg had his sharp blade out and the monster said, "You will never defeat me."

He said, "Yes I will!"

The monster had her weapons - her finger nails and Greg had his sword. They both dodged and deflected each other's attacks until they both got tired. Greg took one more powerful slash and she was too tired to stop it. It sliced through her and she was dead. He noticed this was her graveyard – her home. She killed over 25,000 people it seemed. He was so angry. He thought it as his fault because she was his daughter.

Mike went up to Greg and thanked him for saving him, "It's not your fault mister and you saved me. Come on, let's get out of here." And they went, a new set of friends.

The Dangerous Forest

By: Ivan

Deeper and deeper into the spooky cave, lived a dangerous monster and the monster's name was Grendel! Everyone said that Grendel was very strong. The cave was next to a forest and there was another cave there as well. The caves were like mazes! They were very dark. So dark that you will need torchlights or you will fall down all the time. In one of those caves, lived a hero and his name was Ivan. The other cave, no one dared to go inside. Both Grendel and Ivan also did not go leave their caves. It's because, they were scared of each other.

One day, something happened and they did left their disgusting, creepy, gloomy caves! They never said a word to each other because Grendel stole Ivan's village. Ivan lived in that village. So Ivan wanted his village back. So they were going to fight! As soon as both Grendel and Ivan saw each other outside of the cave, they began to fight each other. It seemed that Grendel was stronger than Ivan.

Grendel's eyes were shining like fire. He was holding a very dangerous sword. The sword was made from the strongest steel in the world and IVAN WAS ONLY HOLDING A STICK! They both came closer and closer to each other and Grendel said to Ivan, "Are you ready to die stick boy?" Ivan did not give an answer!

They were watching each other very seriously with their creepy eyes! Ivan could not wait any longer, he just wanted to fight. So Ivan attacked. He ran to Grendel and stared at him but Grendel did not move! So Ivan had to make a plan.

Ivan ran to Grendel again and Grendel discovered that Ivan's stick was not just a stick. It was a magical stick. The stick was on fire, it burnt Grendel's skin! Grendel paused. He was so scared that he did not even try to scratch to Ivan. Then Ivan cut Grendel's arm off, his leg off, his head off but Grendel was still alive … you cannot defeat evil such as Grendel.

Legend of Kohan

By: Jeremiah

In the depths of the spirit world, a creature, a spirit, a monster, swirled inside a tree, waiting for something, the summer solstice. It was the only time Vaatu, who is the being inside the tree, can roam the Earth. On the other side of a portal, which takes you to the spirit world, a boy in a black and gold robe arose from his slumber. Every morning, the boy would chant, "I am Kohan, Son of May and Kion."

Kohan would fix his green, luscious, emerald hair and smile at himself in the mirror. He would always say, "Good morning Republic City."

And the city would respond with: "Morning Kohan."

In the blink of an eye, a tentacle, as dark as night, reached out of the spirit portal. It was Vatuu! No one had fought Vatuu before so they all evacuated except Kohan. He jumped off his forty-story apartment building to try to land a punch on Vaatu to save the city. Watching this, Ravaa flew over to Kohan to try to save him but accidentally merged with Kohan! All of a sudden, Vatuu shouted. "How dare you Raava, Unala-!"

"YOU MADE A DEAL WITH MY UNCLE!!" Kohan roared with rage, "CURSE YOU VATUU!"

With anger and rage, Kohan ran to the building where his uncle lived until he realised he was not even touching the floor, he was flying! He looked at his hand – he was flying and his hand was burning, emerald green. He looked forward again to a glass building and fell unconscious.

Two hours later, he woke up in a bed with his uncle sitting next to him. With anger surging through his veins, he threw his uncle out the window. Watching this, Vaatu sprang into action and merged with Kohan's uncle.

Kohan jumped out of the window and punched the merged Vatuu across the globe. Kohan had won!! Or did he ...

The Tale of Kayden Uzumaki

By: Kayden

Not very ago, there lived a boy, training to be a true ninja, and he went by the name Kayden Uzumaki. In that time, there was a monster on the loose and this monster went by the name Wrath. Wrath had stolen the forbidden infinity ring and Kayden was determined to return it. He was young foolish and a bit *too* courageous, and he knew this, but he always tried to use this to his advantage. He passed different lands, every once in a while taking an hour to rest or take a nap until, finally, he reached Wrath's den.

Kayden sensed this monsters aura. It was strong; stronger than anything he had ever felt before, but this just got him more fired up. Wrath shot a tentacle out at Kayden and it hit him right in his ninja headband. Wrath shot out another tentacle and it hit Kayden in his belly. He was angry now. The great warrior had fought in many battles before in which he gained his six scars, and now they were glowing. Kayden felt power, and he said, "I am Kayden Uzumaki, this world is where I grew up and I will not let you destroy it! Sharengun!" Sharengun, the forbidden martial arts, Kayden had mastered it! A big ball of purple energy swirled around the cave; however, the power was too much for Kayden or Wrath. The blow split them forty, maybe fifty metres apart from each other. For Kayden, he had learnt how to control this strange power inside of him. All the ninja in training had to do was concentrate his entire mind on this power. This power inside him was a nine-tailed fox that went by the name Korouma. Once he had transformed into Korouma, he used the water martial arts from the power of the nine tails and swiftly came in back into battle. "Final Blowwww!" Kayden bellowed, and Korouma smashed down on Wrath.

The last thing the petrified monster saw was the determined face of Kayden Uzumaki, and right before this new wave of power hit him, Wrath thought to himself, "This boy is destined to stop all things that come in his way, he is the light of the world …"

The Volcano Creature

By: Mahabhir

Far, far, away in the volcano that looked like the door of hell, was creature named Slenderman. He had no eyes and a face of pure white.

A boy, named Sasuke, was training near this volcano and heard a mysterious sound, so he went in to check on what was happening. Skulls lined the edged of the volcano and were dipping in lava. He found Slenderman standing there, still. "Who are you and why are you here?" the creature bellowed.

Sasuke pulled his lighting ball weapon out and put it through Slenderman's stomach. He fell in the lava but he was still alive.

"I am Slenderman and nobody can defeat me because I have

the power of darkness. Where are you from young man? I am from the shadow world and you can't destroy my village!"

Slenderman grabbed Sasuke with its arms. "Who do you think you are?"

"The one who's gonna stop you!" Sasuke yelled at him.

Sasuke went as mad as a lightning. Slenderman was shocked at this anger. The boy grabbed Slenderman and said, "Don't you ever dare to attack my village again!" He chopped off Slenderman's head off.

THE SHADOW LEGEND

By: Maikel

Kakashi and Maikel were in a shadowy, dark cave. That cave was evil. There were dead corpses on the ground. Kakashi lived there and he was the darkest man Maikel had ever seen. Maikel was a good guy. He had white hair. He was the master of the village and now there he was fighting the legend.

They were staring at each other and it was the day to destroy Kakashi. Kakashi began the fight and threw himself into Maikel with his sword but unluckily, it only hit Kakashi's arm.

Maikel threw himself at Kakashi again, but Kakashi dodged Maikel's attack. Maikel, in his mind, remembered that Kakashi's weakness was light; Maikel will be the one who will destroy Kakashi.

Maikel will end this forever. Maikel made a portal on the wall and pushed Kakashi inside that large portal. The creature was a bit weak now and he was finally destroyed.

The End of Suffering

By: Wareesha

Peeking in the shadows, just on the edge of mighty Hall Heorot was an awful place.

It was a dark scary night, in a forest of doom. It was a very foggy day. The wind was howling as soft as a cloud, and the lightning flashed violently while grass swished side to side. Skeletal trees were moving back and forth. A murder of crows was squawking loudly.

Past the skeletal trees were two enormous rocks (with points as sharp daggers) and in the middle of them, was a poisonous pool made with blood which if you go in to, you will die.

And now from that place of doom, a creature emerged …

A pair of glowing red eyes appeared. The eyes pierced the thick fog. It was tall and fat and it loomed over all the evil creatures because it was so tall. It hissed so loud that the animals started making their noises. The animals started moving backwards because they were scared. The giant started yawning so loud that the animals went into their dens.

As the monster started walking towards Hall Heorot, the Blood man started to look for it to confront it.

"Give me all you got," said the monster.

The Blood man replied, "Prepare to die."

The Blood man attacked the monster but was wounded. He raised his sword and pierced the monster's hand. It went right through. And then, the monster tried many times to kill the Blood man but it failed. The Blood man had won.

Almost immediately, the sky illuminated on the forest with a brilliant, bright. The sounds of the demons, vampires and witches were all gone and now the forest is peaceful.

A River of Blood

By: Ramino

It was a gloomy forest that no one went to. It was so creepy that even the trees were speaking and they spoke of the fear that they felt.

Behind the two vast willow trees, was a pool of blood and a stream. This stream, was no ordinary one, it was full of blood and veins. It was almost like this was a river which led to the gateway to hell.

This stream started bubbling and a head that looked like the devil emerged. It popped out and the eyes, the eyes were pink rimmed. The forest creatures that were near got scared and ran the other way. This thing was chasing something. This creatures name was Veined and it was talked about in the legends.

Veined moved and it left a stream of blood behind it and it was breathing in tiny little gasps as if it were choking on all the blood it drank. It was looking for something, sniffing the air and letting out little snarls and hisses.

There was only one man that could stop Veined and that one man was Beowulf. He had defeated many other horrors and he could do it again.

Beowulf had big broad shoulders and he looked bigger sitting down than standing up. He was the kindest person you would ever meet, always paying attention to you and trying to solve your problems, no matter how big or how small.

One day Beowulf went to the woods to hunt for that beast and their paths crossed. Beowulf said, "You shall pay for the bad deeds you've done!"

Veined retorted, "You shall pay for all the good you've done mortal!"

With that, the fight began and they both lunged at each other. Beowulf slashed Veined's wing off with his shiny sword. However, Veined was able to hide himself in smoke which was toxic. He did this and then whipped Beowulf off his feet. Beowulf landed but then quickly bounced back up, holding his breath. He lunged for Veined's head and chopping it off with a mighty swing of his sword.

Veined's head rolled to the ground and Beowulf collected it, taking it with him back to town to show everyone the deed which he had accomplished.

From then on, the forest was peaceful and the river of blood faded to normal water. Peace had been restored.

Alia and the Monster

By: Maryam

Hi I am Alia. I am thirteen today and you wouldn't believe the terrifying day I had. Ok, let's start from the beginning. I was outside collecting my favourite berries when I heard a scream of fear and fright. I was terrified and ran deep in the gloomy, abandoned woods. When I was in the middle of the middle of the spooky woods, I saw a monster with razor sharp claws and a blood thirsty mouth. I was screaming with fear, I thought I was going to die.

I saw blood pools and rotting skeletons everywhere. I was hoping it was a dream but I was wrong. Then, the monster attacked me he ran towards me trying to kill me. I was lucky as dodged almost every move he threw at me. Then, I attacked the monster in his black and red eyes. He was furious and punched me in the stomach. I fell down in pain. He was about to hit me again and I struggled to get up but I found a shiny, silver sword next to me. As he was about to hit me, I stabbed him in the heart and he tried to strike back but was too weak to move and fell down in pain – slowly dying in pain. I ran out of the woods for fear of dying. I had finally reached home and my mum saw me crying and embraced me tight and tucked me in bed. I was glad to be home, just me, mum and my brother.

Even though I escaped and made it home to those who love me, I still have nightmares of that monster.

Cc50 vs Great Greg

By: Piini

Greg was a normal guy with ADD (lack of concentration) who lives in a 4 story house on a hill that was owned by his sister. He always helped people even though he needed help himself so people called him Great Greg.

Greg was on a mission, on a mission to defeat a creature as wicked as a witch and as sly as a fox that haunted his phenomenal family for years. The creature's name was Cc50.

Cruel Cc50 was a sly and huge like an elephant. He was a spirit warrior. Although Cc50 already sounds petrifying, that is not the worst of him. Cc50's humongous hair was poisonous so if you ever touched it, you would die instantly. Cc50 also had flaming, bold eyes that give you the thought of death without even looking into them.

When Greg arrived at the derelict, haunted graveyard, he went up to Cc50's grave and let out his spirit once again.

"What are you doing here? I thought all your family was dead! Who knew some were left..." Cc50 muttered.

Greg charged at Cc50 and BOOM! Blood rushed out of Cc50's leg like a fountain. The enraged spirit ran, jumped, screamed, and lashed out at Greg and punched him so hard that Greg nearly passed out.

Cc50 decided to use his strongest power, the power that made him win every battle of his life, mind controlling. Greg knew that Cc50 could mind control but he didn't care, if he was going to win this battle, he was going to use his outer strength and his inner strength. Greg had lost control of his body and started to attack himself!

"Shallam Shara Shabean!" Greg yelled.

Then, there was silence. A silence so deafening that it had to be broken.

Cc50 made Greg scream in agony as he made Greg harm himself so much that Greg eventually passed out. When Greg woke up, he was surrounded by fire, his hands were full of water and he was floating. He attacked Cc50 and put his hair aflame.

"Loser! You thought you were strong? Too bad, too sad!" teased Greg as he got his elemental powers flowing through him. Cc50 teleported behind Greg and strangled him when suddenly, Cc50 choked on water and he disappeared. Years passed and Cc50 never retured. Greg was unsure exactly if he had defeated the monster. He would be ready though if that beast ever returned to try and harm him again.

Seaman vs Furious Beast

By: Arav

Lurking in the shadows, just on the edge of the mighty Hall Heorot, was a woeful, horrid place. It was a dark, frightful forest that was permanently enveloped in red mist. The wind roared seethingly, lightning flashed from behind the clouds and scorched the ground. The forest was filled with naked, skeletal trees that swished in the bitter wind. Their branches were filled with murders of crows squawking and pecking the trees when anyone dared enter. Mysterious eyes peeked from the shadows whilst cackles and shrieks echoed all around.

And it was from this place of death and despair that the most vile and foul creature ever known to humans, emerged...

A pair of red, devil, bloodshot eyes, which burned with fury, pierced the red mist. Standing more than eleven feet tall, it loomed over all the horrendous, repellent creatures of the fen that had not yet fled. It snarled and hissed from its wide mouth that was filled with rows of pointy, crooked teeth which it used to tear its victims in half. Blood and veins oozed from its scummy lips. Its breath stank like a sewer.

The creature was known as Furious Beast and it crept and slithered towards Hall Heorot. As the beast was moving, Seaman, a great hero, trudged fiercely to confront the monster. Their paths were destined to cross.

"I am worse than darkness!" hissed and declared Furious Beast. "Prepare to meet your maker you dumb, floppy human." Without a single word, Seaman calmly drew his trident out of his scabbard and posed to get ready for battle. "Give me all you got, you hideous monstrosity," Furious Beast roared. Seaman's trident glowed gold and its point was as sharp as a dagger. His face was filled with scars and braveness. He stood as still as a statue.

Furious Beast moved hypersonic like a cheetah. His sword was made of magma and shone orange. They both got out to the battlefield and ran to fight. Their trident and sword clashed against each other. Furious Beast trusted himself and attacked again and broke Seaman's shield into hundreds of pieces.

Seaman was filled with rage and attacked. He broke half of Furious Beast's sword and laughed. "I'll break your sword even more and you'll have nothing to fight with."

But then Furious Beast got angrier and bellowed, "Bring it

on!" They kept fighting and clashing their swords and then suddenly Furious Beast knocked Seaman off his feet. Furious Beast dragged Seaman around until Seaman kicked him in his face and Furious Beast's one tooth fell out. His mouth was filled with blood.

Furious Beast ran away crying, "I'll come get you next time you bully seaman!" He pretended his was a coward and fleeing, but then quickly turned at Seaman and grinned. He had tricked Seaman. Furious Beast jumped at Seaman with hypersonic speed again and they started clashing swords until Seaman managed to stick his trident into Furious Beast's neck and his head fell off.

Furious Beast would not bother anyone anymore.

THE ANGEL VS THE DEMON

By: Iuliana

Lurking far from Hall Heorot was a scary, deep, dark forest. There were loads of skeleton trees with black birds that sounded so loud and looked so disgusting. There had been such loud cracking of thunder that you could die from how loud it was. As you stared into the woods, it felt like you were looking at people because there were eyes and shadows of heads everywhere.

You could not dare yourself to go there because under the leaves on the floor were loads of sharp rocks. As well, you could see some beasts fishing in a disgusting putrid river. You could not see too far though because of the fog. The moon gave a little light and a witch could be seen riding her broomstick.

Out of the putrid river came a scary creature named Bloody

Face. He was ugly and his body was covered in blood and slime. He was very fat and his house in the middle of the woods looked like the entrance to HELL! His eyes were like bloody-fire, his nails were longer than a sword. Its long spiky wings were made out of fire. Its long, long tail could catch anything. It could even catch the animals from the highest trees ever in the world.

As Bloody Face started to crawl out of the forest to find some people to eat, he found Wolf Power. As Wolf Power heard that everyone hated Bloody Face so as soon as he saw him he said, "I'll fight you beast! No one likes you so I'll get rid of you for everyone!"

"I am worse than darkness!" furiously shouted Bloody Face. "You want to get rid of me!? It is I who will get rid of you! You shall never see the light again!"

"I am good and I am light, you shall never see dark again and never see yourself!" Wolf Power said confidently. Some seconds later, Bloody Face showed his power and took out his sword and shield and then the fight began.

Wolf Power used his power and broke Blood Face's shield and someone took Bloody Face's attention and then Wolf Power took out his sword and smashed it.

Because Wolf Power did that, Bloody Face started to go on Wolf Power and in a blink of an eye, Wolf Power was on top of Bloody Face. After that, Wolf Power stabbed Bloody Face with bits of the broken sword.

At last, the fight ended and Wolf Power had won. As they were fighting for the forest, Wolf Power won and the forest became the best place to be in.

The Malfunction Robot

By: Marcus

I stepped foot into the battle arena. I walked over to the outskirts of the arena and sat down.

"And with the hit!" I hear a voice echoing out form the speakers overhead, "Darkvanish hits Litenight off the centre and falls into the acid below, finishing him!" I realised it was the announcer of the games, talking through the speakers.

"Now for the next challengers, Lemour Lord and Mommy Anespid!" His voice was so loud you could hear it everywhere and there I was sitting, waiting patiently for my turn.

"And with a strike, Mommy Anespid defeats Lemour Lord! Now, it's time for our tenth battle for the evening. It's time for …" I knew this was my turn so I picked up my stuff and got ready. It was time to battle. "… Bloodkill and Deathsound to step into the arena!"

I walked into that huge arena and waited. I looked over to my opponent, Deathsound, and saw something was wrong. My opponent, unexpectantly, wasn't human. So inhuman in fact, that it looked like something from a horror story.

I was so shocked that I hadn't realised that the battle started. My 'opponent' or whatever you want to call that thing, shot an entire flaming ball of hot melted gunk at me and it nearly hit me. I swung my sword at it and my weapon burst into flames, melting onto the ground. I dodged that attack, but for how long could I hold out against this beast? I shot my bow and arrow and missed the creature. I remembered that my aim with bows was terrible so I forgot that idea and looked for another weapon.

Near a rock, I found a ball and chain and swung it over towards the creature, stabbing it in the eye. It let out a blood curdling scream. Now I know why it was called Deathsound. I don't know exactly what happened but I looked away and turned back to see a gooey, black, giant robot where my opponent had been.

I remembered that this clearly wasn't an ordinary fight and looked up to see the creature was inside the robot. How? Why? There was no time to figure out exactly what had happened. It was either fight or be killed and I quite like living.

I was fearless. I was going to save the city from this creature no matter what. I had to do this. It was do or die time.

The Family in the Dark Forest

By: Amina

One day in dark forest there was trees and the monsters are hiding behind the trees the monsters coming slowly in the darkness to eat small monsters one day there was one family in dark forest and from the family the girls whole body was covered in blood and monster smell it, the monster came to eat girl when the girl is dead the monster came to eat her when the monster eats after the monster bite the girls leg.

The family say what this noise tom went to saw when the tom saw the monster just eating the girl when the monster ate the girl the monster saw tom and the monster jumped on tom and monster bit it.

But one day they did something to kill the monster the next day the mom did something to kill the monster and the lily kill small monster to take some blood and lily took a glass to put the blood inside the glass lily hide the glass the monster smell it and the monster and when monster eat it and the monster dead.

One day there is one more monster, the monster coming slowly to lily and the monster smell the blood the monster ran away and lily ran away to sit in her car and the monster saw lily jump in the car and the lily ran out from the car.

Next day there are 10 small monsters and lily needs blood to kill all the monsters and lily kills all the small monsters and she fills all the blood in the glass she mixes something to kill the monsters and lily hides the glass when all the monster sees there is blood when the monsters eat the blood.

The next day lilies all the body is dirty lily get some water to wash her body when she wash her body and there is one monster lily can't do anything to kill the monster and lily throw the stone to kill the monster and lily just throwing the stone and lily throw the stone in her eyes and lily finding the small monster to take some blood to kill the monster and lily find one small monster and lily took something to kill and she put the blood inside the glass and she mixes something to kill the monster lily hides the glass when the monster smell it the monster run away.

Lily go to car when she saw her car the monsters broke her car and lily is crying how she gonna go to her house and lily don't have phone to call anyone and next day there is one girl lily is so happy she find one girl.

The Beast

By: Daiyan

Within the depth of the black dark fen, there was a beast. This beast was the Deathound. It was a deadly beast and everyone feared him until one day, a hero came.

In The Land of The Danes, there was a man named Theodore. Theodore was a bright young man with a big heart and he had heard about the monster, so he wanted to defeat it.

He set off on his camel, thinking of his mission. He travelled over deserts, mountains and rivers then he found it, the monster, the evil Deathound.

As he pulled out his dazzling diamond sword, the worst thing happened. Deathound's was bloodred with fury. It was ready to tear anyone or anything apart.

Theodore rushed into Deathhouse. "Oh no," he thought, thinking he would die. He continued to slash and soon he realised it only peeled off the skin from the monster's body. Then, the monster attacked and injured his arm badly. Theodore jerked back into the light. He soon realised the monster hated sunlight so he ran to the back of the beast and kicked him straight into the sunlight. Slowly but surely it turned to stone. He then broke off the head and took it with him.

By the time he got back home, the news had spread out about his heroism. Soon after, King Hoska gave Theodore the crown and he became King of the Danes. Everybody loved him.

The Toilet Monster

By: Rafay

There once was a boy named Jack. He was thirteen years old and in eighth grade. He was a naughty kid who always got into trouble with his 'pranks.' The one thing he enjoyed doing most was messing with the toilets.

Here's what happened.

"I'm gonna play a prank on Rafay. I'm gonna flush so much toilet paper into the toilet that when he goes to use it, it will explode everywhere!" Jack said to Muhammad.

"You really shouldn't do that to Rafay. That wouldn't be nice. He's the new kid after all. Maybe we can prank someone else today Jack. Maybe even a teacher!"

"No Muhammad. I want to make the toilet explode on Rafay, so that's what we are going to do."

Muhammad sighed. He knew that once Jack set his mind to something, there was no stopping it. Poor Rafay was going to get covered in toilet water.

Together, Muhammad and Jack started to push lots of toilet paper into the toilet. Muhammad brought it and Jack stuffed it down. "That will do. When Rafay comes to flush, BOOM! Hahahahaha!"

A little while later, Rafay arrived at school and Jack and Muhammad hid around the corner, waiting to see what would happen. It was weird though, as Rafay went in, everyone else was running out of the toilets, screaming. There was a toilet monster!

Rafay was already in the toilet, so he hid in one of the stalls. He hoped that the monster wouldn't find him there. Rafay was climbing up onto the toilet so that the monster couldn't see his feet from underneath. He accidentally flushed …

BOOM!

SPLASH!

Water went everywhere. Rafay came flying out of the toilets covered in toilet water and tissue. Jack and Muhammad were laughing so hard at him until the toilet monster came out of the bathroom. It saw the two boys pointing and laughing and it ran at them.

Rafay may have been covered in toilet water that day, but Jack and Muhammad, the bullies, were never seen again.

Printed in Great Britain
by Amazon

63727408R00043